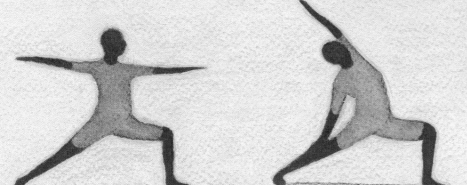

Nothando's Journey

Acknowledgments:
Thank you to the people of Swaziland for the kind, hospitable, open,
loving, and joyful spirit you shared with me. May Nothando's story
continue to inspire children everywhere.

Dedication:
... to the children of Swaziland
... to my children, Christina, Dana, John, and Ron
... to children everywhere

May your discovery of yourself bring you a strong sense of clarity,
peace within, and well-being.

©2016 TEXT JILL APPERSON MANLY — ©2016 ILLUSTRATIONS ALYSSA CASEY

Published by
Jabu Kids, Corona Del Mar, CA

ISBN 13: 978-0-615-89235-1

LCCN: 2015936250

Design by Yvonne Fetig Roehler

Printed in the United States by Worzalla Publishing, First Printing, November 2015
19   18   17   16   15   •   5   4   3   2   1

NOTHANDO'S JOURNEY

BY **JILL APPERSON MANLY**

ILLUSTRATIONS BY **ALYSSA CASEY**

JABU KIDS ~ CORONA DEL MAR, CA

Jabu and Nothando live in Swaziland,
a place of rolling hills and stretching plains.

The sun shines bright on villages of families and a countryside full of lions that roar and baboons that play.

Today is the Reed Festival, a special day in Swaziland, and a special day for Nothando.

For the first time she will join the other girls in the country to dance in front of the King and Queen Mother.

Her brother, Jabu, helps Nothando get ready.
He ties on an anklet made of dried pods,

which she will stomp and rattle to the songs
sung by the girls at the Reed Festival.

Jabu knows Nothando is nervous
about the dance and the long journey.

"Should we walk through the hills
or the valley?" asks Jabu.
"The path over the hills is shorter,
but we've never gone that way before."

Nothando is afraid of what lies
over the unknown hills,
but she does not want to be late.

So the two siblings start the long walk
out of the village up into the hills.

Along the path, they meet a wild dog.

"Oh no!" says Nothando.

She is scared of wild dogs,
with their deep growls and big teeth.

"Don't be scared, Nothando," says Jabu.

"Look, the dog is just stretching
and enjoying the sun.
Come on, Nothando,
you try it," encourages Jabu.

9

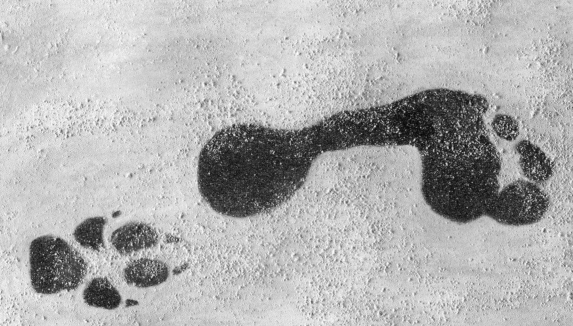

Nothando stretches in the sun.
The stretch comforts her tired legs and back.

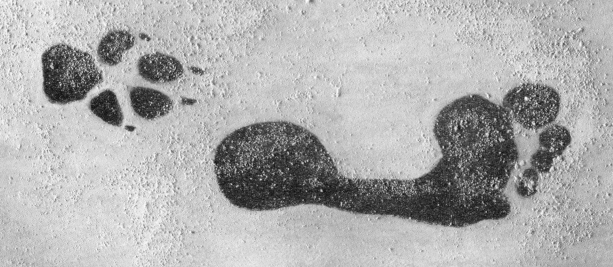

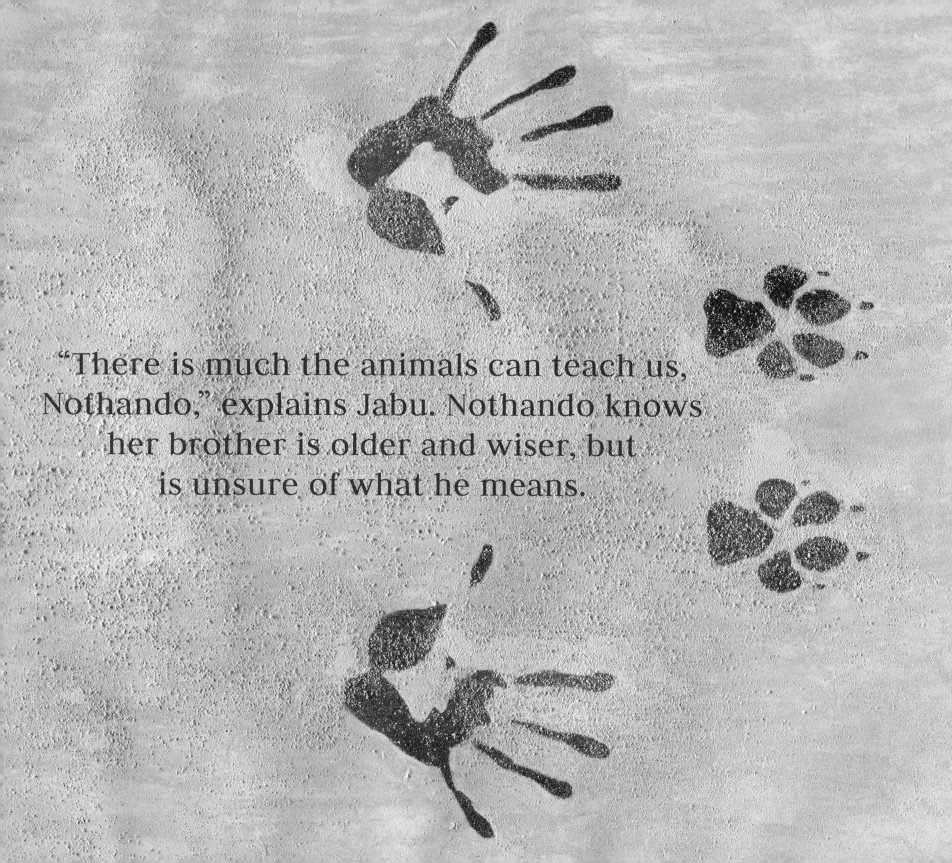

"There is much the animals can teach us, Nothando," explains Jabu. Nothando knows her brother is older and wiser, but is unsure of what he means.

As the sun rises higher overhead,
they begin to feel thirsty and tired.
They decide to rest at the top of the hill
beside the great baobab tree.

Below them, on the other side of the hill,
is a surprising sight.

"Jabu, look! Lions! Baboons! Cobras!
Fish eagles! Wild dogs! And even elephants!
All together at the watering hole!
They must have been thirsty, too."

Nothando remembers the stretch of the wild dog

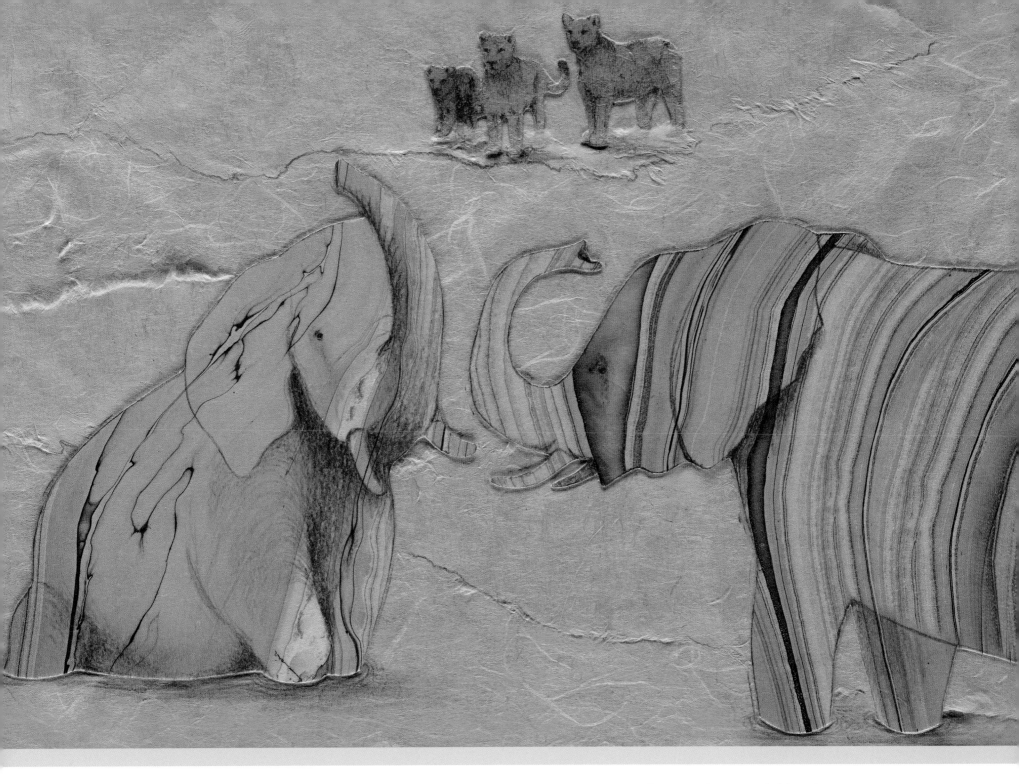

and is curious what the other animals will do.

Nothando spots the prints
of a baby elephant.

She steps next to them and playfully swings her arms.

"Look, Jabu!
I am steady like an elephant,"
states Nothando.

Jabu smiles.

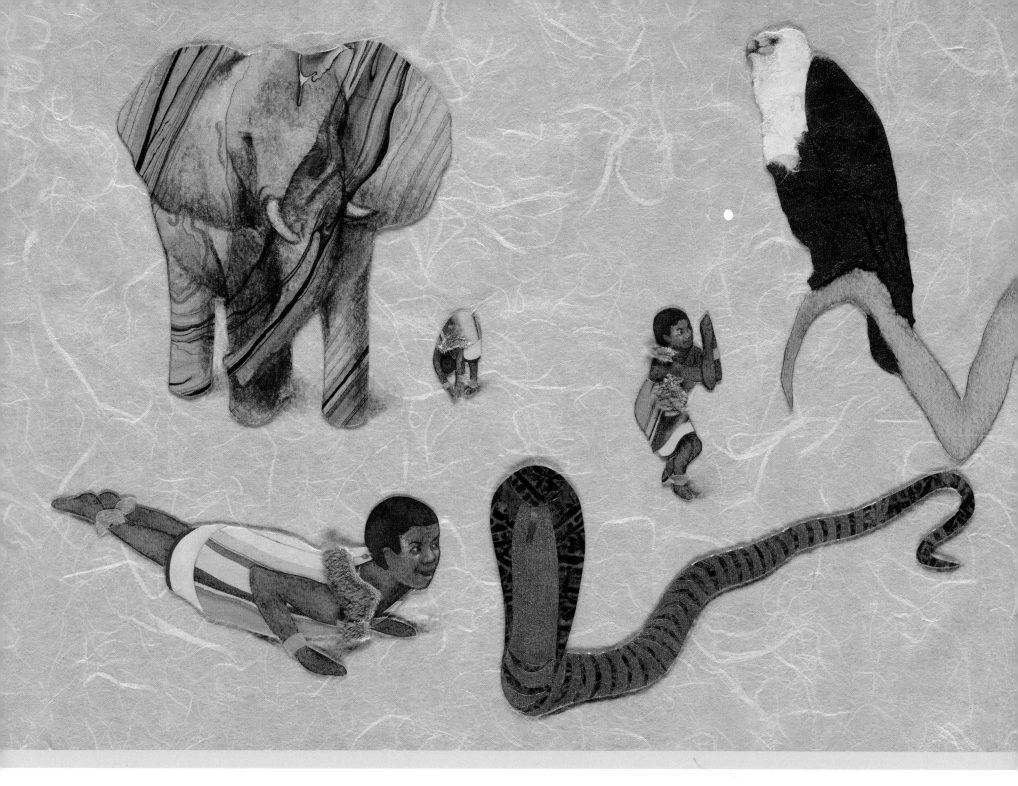

He knows Nothando is learning from the animals.

She feels as strong as a lion.

She feels as calm as a fish eagle.

She feels as brave as a baboon.

28

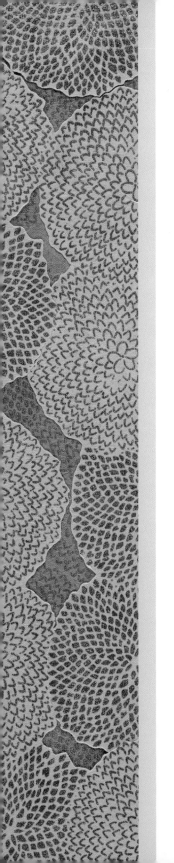

By observing and moving like the animals,
Nothando has learned many new things
about herself.

She is no longer afraid to dance
before the King or Queen Mother.

She is excited to dance with the other Swazi girls.

Nothando now has courage, playfulness,
and strength all inside of her.

She is grateful to be Nothando.

Nothando and Jabu hear the singing,
whistles, and shouts coming from the valley.

The Reed Festival is about to begin.

Nothando leaves the watering hole
refreshed, happy, and wiser.

She whispers a small thanks
to the animals at the watering hole
before running down the hill.

31

The proud girls begin

to dance across the field.

Nothando is ready to join her first Reed Festival.

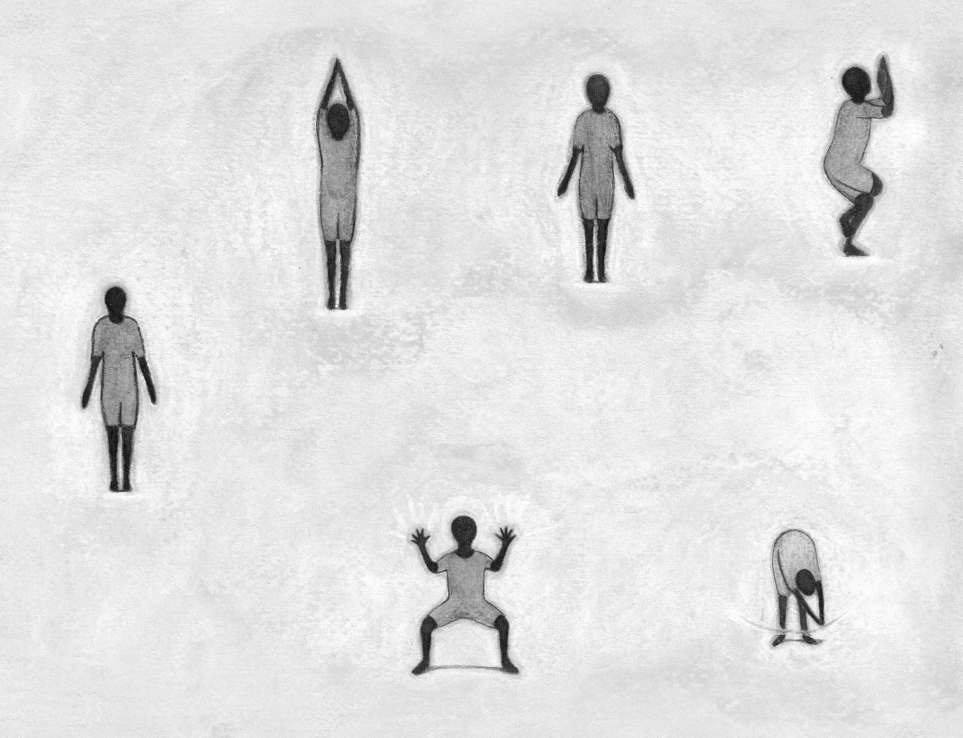